TONY JOHNSTON

The Magic Maguey

Illustrated by Elisa Kleven

HARCOURT BRACE & COMPANY   San Diego   New York   London

Requests for permission to make copies of any part of
the work should be mailed to: Permissions Department,
Harcourt Brace & Company, 6277 Sea Harbor Drive, Orlando, Florida 32887-6777.

Library of Congress Cataloging-in-Publication Data

Johnston, Tony, 1942–

The magic maguey/written by Tony Johnston; illustrated by Elisa Kleven.—1st ed.

p.   cm.

Summary: Miguel figures out a way to save the beloved maguey plant in his Mexican pueblo.

ISBN 0-15-250988-7

[1. Agave—Fiction.   2. Mexico—Fiction.   3. Christmas—Fiction.]

I. Kleven, Elisa, ill.   II. Title.

PZ7.J6478Maj   1996

[Fic]—dc20   94-32660

First edition   A B C D E

Printed in Singapore

The illustrations in this book were done in mixed-media collage,

using watercolors, pastels, and cut paper.

The display type and text type were set in Kennerly by

Harcourt Brace & Company Photocomposition Center, San Diego, California.

Color separations by Bright Arts, Ltd., Singapore

Printed and bound by Tien Wah Press, Singapore

This book was printed with soya-based inks on Leykam recycled paper,

which contains more than 20 percent postconsumer waste

and has a total recycled content of at least 50 percent.

Production supervision by Warren Wallerstein and Pascha Gerlinger

Designed by Camilla Filancia

For Stella and Ernesto Amtmann,

who know the maguey is magical,

and for Suzi, my little dog

—T. J.

For Susan, Gail, and Kay

—E. K.

ONCE long ago a boy named Miguel lived in a pueblo in Mexico. Miguel lived with his mother and father in a small adobe house. He had helped his father make the adobe bricks of clay and water and straw.

Down the dirt road from where Miguel lived there was an enormous plant. It grew on the land of Don César, a very rich man indeed. Its dust green leaves reached to the sky like a huge, spiky bouquet. The plant was called maguey.

The people of the pueblo liked the maguey. The men and women met there to gossip and chat. The children played there in the sun. And in the rain. Even the little dogs went there to nose around.

Every day Miguel passed the maguey on his way to school. *Slap, slap, slap* went his *chanclas*, his sandals, as he walked along.

He stopped beside the maguey.

"Buenos días," he told it. "Good morning."

He skipped around it. Then he hurried on.

After school he sat in the shade of the maguey to do his lessons.
He played there with his friends, Lupita and Chayo and Juan.

The sun sank like a cactus bloom.

Then they all waved. *"Hasta mañana, maguey."* "See you tomorrow."

And they went home.

Miguel thought the maguey was the best plant in the world.

When he and his father were building their adobe, his father
had said, "The maguey is *una maravilla,* a marvel. See what it can do."

Father had collected many of its old leaves. He took a big knife.
He sliced the tough leaves into pieces the size of *tejas,* the red clay
tiles on the roofs of the other houses.

He had climbed to the top of their adobe. Carefully, he placed the
maguey pieces there, overlapping like small green hills.

"Magic!" his father had said. "The maguey is now a roof!"

"Magic!" Miguel cried.

Sometimes Miguel's mother passed the maguey on her way to market. If a leaf had fallen off, she put it into her shopping *canasta* and brought it home like a great green vegetable.

With a sharp knife she removed the strings inside. She washed them and dried them in the sun. She wound them on a dry corncob. Then she made a shirt for Miguel, stitched with maguey string.

"Magic!" she said when he put the shirt on. "Now the maguey is thread!"

"Magic!" cried Miguel.

Now it was Christmastime in the pueblo. Everybody felt happy. People decorated their houses inside and out.

Miguel and his family decorated their adobe.

In old cans his mother planted *nochebuenas*, poinsettias, like red flames. They hung ornaments everywhere—straw stars and angels and donkeys, gaily painted clay bells and camels and kings, little lumpy lambs of yarn, small piñatas, and doves, doves, *doves*. Each ornament was hung with maguey thread.

Night came, spreading her black shawl over all. Mother lit candles inside the adobe. The candles glittered like stars. The family was ready for Christmas.

"Miguel?" his mother asked one day.

"¿Sí, mamá?"

"Please go to buy tamales from Doña Josefa."

She poured some coins into his hand.

"Sí, mamá," Miguel said eagerly.

He loved Doña Josefa's tamales, some yellow and filled with meat, some light and pink and sweet.

He put the coins in his pocket and hurried off.

Slap, slap, slap sang his *chanclas* on the road. *Clink, clink, clink* sang the coins.

He came to the big maguey.

Some men were ringed around it, pointing and talking all at once. Don César spoke loudest of all.

Miguel heard him say, "Now you are too busy with Christmas to work one little minute. But when Christmas has passed, you must chop down this ugly maguey. Then I will build a fine house here. *That* will be something to look at."

Miguel could not believe what he heard.

The beautiful maguey that had been there forever. The magic maguey would be gone!

He no longer cared about tamales. He no longer cared about Christmas.

Slowly, he walked home. His *chanclas* made no sound.

"*¿Qué tienes, m'ijo?*" his mother asked when he came in. "What is wrong, my son?"

Quietly he told her. Then he lay down on his *petate,* the mat that was his bed.

There was nothing else to do.

When they heard the news of the maguey, the people gathered there. Everybody spoke at once. But nobody knew what to do. The beautiful old plant did not mean *papas*, potatoes, to Don César. What mattered was his very fine house.

Days passed. And nights passed. Christmas came closer.
Miguel thought of the maguey all the time. But he did not know how
to save it.

On Christmas Eve his mother lit the candles in the adobe. They
sparkled like sugar on Christmas cookies. They glittered like stars.
All of the ornaments shone.

Miguel stared at the candles. And the shining ornaments.

He had an idea at last!

When his mother and father were asleep, he slipped out into the night.

"*Hssst! Hssst! Hssst!*" Miguel whispered at the windows of his friends. "Chayo! Lupita! Juan! *¡Levántense!* Get up!"

The friends got up. Many friends got up. They listened to Miguel. They whispered. And giggled. And whispered some more.

Then—

Sssh, sssh, sssh. Many *chanclas* tiptoed down the road.

And then—like many Santa Clauses, Miguel and his friends hung angels and stars and small piñatas and donkeys and bells and camels and kings and doves, doves, *doves.* They set candles on the curving maguey leaves. Candles in holders like nests of tin.

When all was ready they lit the candles. They glittered like stars.

Then Miguel and his friends began to sing. They sang and sang.

People in their houses woke up.

"What is that?" they asked. They peeked out to see.

Soon everybody gathered around the big maguey. Even the little dogs. Even Don César.

Soon everybody was singing. Even Don César. Even the little dogs.

Miguel whispered to his mother and father, "Magic! The maguey is a Christmas tree!"

"Magic!" They agreed.

When the songs were over, Don César coughed a lot.
"This place is not good for a fine house," he said. "It is not good
for anything, really—except a big maguey."

Everybody cheered and sang once more. Miguel sang loudest of all.
Everybody stayed up too late. Even the little dogs.

And nobody cared.